Recognizing Patterns in Nature

Tony Hyland

Real World Math Books are published by Capstone Press,
151 Good Counsel Drive, P.O. Box 669, Mankato, Minnesota 56002.
www.capstonepub.com

032010
005740CGF10

Books published by Capstone Press are manufactured with paper
containing at least 10 percent post-consumer waste.

Library of Congress Cataloging-in-Publication Data
Hyland, Tony.
  Recognizing patterns in nature / by Tony Hyland.—1st hardcover ed.
    p. cm.—(Real world math level 4)
  Includes index.
  ISBN 978-1-4296-5242-1 (library binding)
  1. Pattern perception. I. Title. II. Series.
  BF294.H95 2011
  152.14'23—dc22   2010001821

Editorial Credits
Sara Johnson, editor; Emily R. Smith, M.A.Ed., editorial director; Sharon Coan, M.S.Ed., editor-in-chief;
Lee Aucoin, creative director; Rachelle Cracchiolo, M.S.Ed., publisher

Photo Credits
The author and publisher would like to gratefully credit or acknowledge the following for permission
to reproduce copyright material: cover Big Stock Photo; pp.1–29 (background) iStock; p.1 iStock; p.4
Shutterstock; p.5 Shutterstock; p.6 Big Stock Photo; p.8 Shutterstock; p.9 (top) Photolibrary.com; p.9
(bottom) Alamy/Colin Craig; p.10 (both) Shutterstock; p.11 Photolibrary.com; p.12 Jupiter Images; p.13
(left) iStock; p.13 (right) Shutterstock; p.14 iStock; p.15 Big Stock Photo; p.16 Photolibrary.com; p. 17 (left)
Big Stock Photo; p.17 (right) Photolibrary.com/Ed Reschke; p.18 iStock; p.19 (both) iStock; p.20 (left)
Jupiter Images; p.20 (right) Shutterstock; p.21 Jupiter Images; p.22 Shutterstock; p.24 Photolibrary.com/
Brian Kenney; p.25 Big Stock Photo; p.26 Photolibrary.com; p.27 Shutterstock; p.28 Photolibrary.com.

Table of Contents

Camp Patton

I was looking out the window with my friends Ramell and Tisha as we drove up in the bus. Camp Patton looked great!

"Hey, Jamie!" called Ramell. "See the lake? There are **canoes** (ka-NEWS) that we can paddle!"

"Cool!" said Tisha.

Mr. Amos, our teacher, did another head-count before we got off the bus.

"It's still 24, Mr. Amos," said Ramell, "12 boys and 12 girls."

We all laughed. Mr. Amos had already counted us 4 times!

LET'S EXPLORE MATH

Mr. Amos counted 24 students by counting 2 groups of 12. There are other ways he could have grouped the children to still count up to 24. Look at the number line.

0 1 2 3 4 5 6 7 8 9 10 11 12 13 14 15 16 17 18 19 20 21 22 23 24

a. What is the next number that will be marked on the line?

b. What is the last number that will be marked on the line?

c. What other groupings could Mr. Amos use?

Settling In

Ethan and Suzi, our **counselors** (KOWN-suh-lers), were waiting to take us to the **bunkhouses**. Ours had 6 beds—3 double bunks.

Ramell raced in and got a top bunk. I wasn't fast enough, so I settled for the one below him.

"Wow!" said Ramell. "Four whole days here."

"Why is this place called Camp Patton?" I asked Ethan.

"It's named after a famous **general**," explained Ethan. "But it's a good name because *Patton* sounds like *pattern*. And, there are plenty of **patterns** to see here."

I looked around the room. There was even a striped pattern on one of the walls.

What Are Patterns?

A pattern is something that is repeated. There are patterns in clothing, in numbers, and even in nature.

LET'S EXPLORE MATH

Look at this number **sequence** (see-KWENZ).

11, 18, 29, 47, 76, ___

a. Which number comes next?

b. What is the rule you followed to find the next number in the sequence?

Getting Ready

After we unpacked our gear, we went up to the main building. Ethan and Suzi told us we would soon be going on our first hike.

Mr. Amos said, "We've been talking about patterns in class. When we go hiking, I want you to look for patterns around you. Take notes, and draw what you see."

Ramell joked, "I see a pattern on Jamie's shirt. Does that count?"

Mr. Amos laughed. "Well, yes, it's a pattern. But I want you to look for patterns on plants, insects, rocks—anything in nature."

Setting Off

After lunch, we set out on our hike. We saw patterns everywhere. Even the clouds formed a pattern.

We walked beside the lake for a while. There were ripples forming a **continuous** (kuhn-TIN-you-us) pattern on the water. Ethan said the ripples were caused by dropping a rock into the lake.

I found a big rock with stripes through it. Suzi said it was sandstone. I drew a picture of it. It was just too big to put into my pocket!

LET'S EXPLORE MATH

Jamie found some flowers. He made a table in his notebook.

a. Draw the table and fill in the missing numbers.

b. What is the rule for the number pattern in Jamie's table?

Number of Flowers and Petals

Flowers	Petals
1	4
2	8
	12
4	

Down by the Lake

We stopped to watch some birds on the lake. Suzi said she could tell they were common loons by the patterns on their backs.

Ramell and I both said, "Patterns?" We quickly drew the loons in our notebooks.

common loons

"What other animals with patterns live around here?" Tisha asked.

"Raccoons, but they mainly come out at night. There are also skunks and chipmunks," answered Suzi.

"Skunks? Eeew!" I cried.

"Chipmunks are so cute!" Tisha said.

raccoon

chipmunk

Patterns in the Stream

We kept walking and came to a stream. The water was shallow and clear. We could see fish. They swam one way, and then suddenly darted another way, and then another. It was like watching a moving **zigzag** pattern.

On the other side of the stream was a high sandstone cliff. There was a pattern of colorful stripes running through the cliff.

Suzi said, "This is where that rock you found at the lake came from, Jamie."

LET'S EXPLORE MATH

Draw the zigzag number trail and finish the number pattern.

Flying High

As we walked across an open field, Mr. Amos pointed to a flock of geese in the sky.

"The birds are flying in a V-shaped pattern," said Tisha.

Mr. Amos said, "That's right. **Migrating** birds fly in this pattern because it saves energy. That way, they can fly farther."

Further on, we saw some milkweed plants. Monarch butterflies fluttered around. They had bright orange wings with a black pattern around the edges.

I turned over some milkweed leaves and found butterfly eggs. They had ridged patterns on them.

butterfly egg

monarch butterfly

LET'S EXPLORE MATH

Flocks of geese often fly in a "V" shape. In the first row there is 1 bird. Then in the second row there are 2 birds. This makes a total of 3 birds. Row 3 has another 2 birds, making a total of 5 birds. *Hint:* Draw a table that shows how many geese are in each row.

a. How many birds would there be if there were 15 rows?

b. How many rows would there be if there were 49 geese?

Into the Woods

Soon, we came to the woods. Tisha spotted a moth on a tree trunk. I don't know how she found it. Its pattern matched the tree bark exactly. Its markings gave it an excellent **camouflage** (KAM-uh-flazh).

The trees were interesting. Ethan and Suzi **recognized** each tree's leaf patterns. There were oak, birch, maple, and ash trees. We drew the leaf shapes and patterns in our notebooks.

Then Mr. Amos smiled. "Let's make a number sequence with the leaves," he said.

So I stood holding 3 leaves. Then Tisha stood next to me holding 8 leaves. Ethan stood next to her holding 13 leaves. Ramell realized that the rule for the number sequence was "add 5" so he stood next to Ethan holding 18 leaves. Our number pattern went on for a few more students. Luckily, there were a lot of leaves in the woods!

LET'S EXPLORE MATH

Look at this number sequence: 28, 25, 22, __, __.

a. What numbers come next in the sequence?

Now look at this number sequence: 96, 48, 24, __, __.

b. What numbers come next in the sequence?

c. How did you work out your answers to **a** and **b**?

A Surprise

    Our hike was nearly over, and we were heading back to camp.

    "Are there any big animals living here, like bears or mountain lions?" Ramell asked.

    "Not in these woods," said Ethan. "And that's good. Big animals can be scary!"

mountain lion

"How about ... getting *skunked*?" I asked. Everyone looked at me.

"Just up there!" I said as I pointed.

"Now that's one pattern I didn't want to see," cried Tisha.

grizzly bear

skunk

The Skunk

The skunk was about 20 yards (18 meters) away, but we could see 2 white stripes running down its back and along its bushy tail. It didn't look happy.

"Stay still and quiet, and it should go away," said Suzi. "It probably has a **den** nearby."

"I'll make it go!" called Ramell. He started to wave his arms in the air.

"No!" whispered Ethan. "If you do that, he'll squirt us for sure."

Ramell dropped his arms and we waited.

LET'S EXPLORE MATH

The 2 stripes on the skunk reminded Jamie of the "stripes" he had seen on a hundred chart at school. Look at this hundred chart. The dark blue column shows the pattern you get when you count by 10s.

0	1	2	3	4	5	6	7	8	9
10	11	12	13	14	15	16	17	18	19
20	21	22	23	24	25	26	27	28	29
30	31	32	33	34	35	36	37	38	39
40	41	42	43	44	45	46	47	48	49
50	51	52	53	54	55	56	57	58	59
60	61	62	63	64	65	66	67	68	69
70	71	72	73	74	75	76	77	78	79
80	81	82	83	84	85	86	87	88	89
90	91	92	93	94	95	96	97	98	99

a. Draw your own hundred chart like the one above. What pattern is made when you count by 11s? *Hint:* Remember to start at 0.

b. What pattern is made when you count by 9s?

Phew!

"Keep still and quiet, everyone," whispered Suzi.

The skunk stared at us and lifted his tail. We all held our breath.

Suddenly, the skunk turned and ran off into the woods.

"Phew! What a relief!" sighed Mr. Amos.

We walked along the trail to where the skunk had been. The air smelled bad.

"If Ramell kept waving his arms, we'd all be smelling like this!" laughed Ethan.

Ramell went red, and looked at some pinecones on the ground. "These have an interesting pattern," he said.

Back at Camp

Back at camp, Mr. Amos looked at the things we had drawn or picked up. He liked the stripy pattern on my rock. But Ramell's pinecone was amazing. Its **spiral** patterns seemed to go in 2 different directions!

We did great things at Camp Patton. We even paddled the canoes. But seeing the striped skunk was the best of all.

Ramell thought his pinecone was best. He does not want to talk about skunks.

LET'S EXPLORE MATH

Look at the pinecone on page 26. It has 21 spirals: 8 going in one direction, 13 going in the other. The numbers 8, 13, and 21 are part of a famous number pattern that you will learn more about on pages 28 and 29. Now complete this number sequence below.

21, 13, 8, ____ , ____

Famous Fibonacci

The Fibonacci (fee-buh-NAH-chee) sequence is a very famous sequence of numbers. This sequence is named after an Italian math expert, Leonardo Pisano Fibonacci. Fibonacci lived from 1170 to 1250.

Fibonacci numbers are a series of numbers. The numbers follow a special pattern. The first 10 numbers in the Fibonacci sequence are:

1, 1, 2, 3, 5, 8, 13, 21, 34, 55.

Solve It!

Now let's see if you can work out the Fibonacci sequence. Here's a small clue to help you!

$1 + 1 = 2$

$1 + 2 = 3$

a. What rule does the Fibonacci sequence follow?

b. Continue the addition pattern for the numbers shown above to show how you worked out your answer.

c. What would be the next 3 numbers in the sequence, after 55?

A Secret Challenge

Now it is your turn to create a secret number code.

d. Work out a number code of your own. Show it to a friend and see if he or she can work out the rule.

Glossary

bunkhouses—simple buildings that have bunks for sleeping

camouflage—to hide something by coloring or covering it to look like something else

canoes—small boats with pointed ends

continuous—nonstop, with no breaks

counselors—people who supervise campers or activities at a camp

den—the hidden home of a wild animal

general—a high-ranking military officer

migrating—moving from one country to another

patterns—a repeated design, using numbers, shapes, colors, etc.

recognized—knew someone or something from before

sequence—a pattern that follows a rule

spiral—a continuous curve moving around fixed points

zigzag—an angled line that goes one way, then turns sharply in the opposite direction, then back the first way and so on

Index

Let's Explore Math

Page 5:
a. 18   **b.** 24   **c.** Groupings of 2s, 3s, 4s, and 8s.

Page 7:
a. 123   **b.** Add the 2 numbers before the next number.

Page 11:
a. 3, 16
b. Multiply by 4

Page 15:

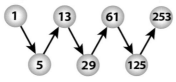

Page 17:
a. 15 rows = 29 geese
b. 49 geese = 25 rows

Page 19:
a. 19, 16   **b.** 12, 6
c. For **a**, subtract 3. For **b**, divide the previous number by 2.

Page 23:
a. A diagonal pattern from left to right is made.
b. A diagonal pattern from right to left is made.

Page 27:
21, 13, 8, 5, 3

Pages 28–29:
Problem-Solving Activity

a. Add the 2 numbers before the next number.
b. $3 + 5 = 8$
$5 + 8 = 13$
$8 + 13 = 21$
$13 + 21 = 34$
$21 + 34 = 55$
c. The next 3 numbers are 89, 144, and 233.
d. Answers will vary.